ABC Disability

SR: For my dearest Willow, Freddie and Andy.
I thank you for riding this journey with me and may
this book make the world a better place.

AP: For Malili, our brightest light.

BF: For my mum, Di, who made me believe
that I could do anything.

ABC Disability

Sarah Rose WITH **Alley Pascoe** ILLUSTRATED BY **Beck Feiner**

LOTHIAN Children's Books

Introduction

Hi friends,

I'm so happy that you've picked up this book. My name is Sarah, and I was born with dwarfism. I am a person of short stature, but I'm also so much more than that. I'm a three-time Paralympic swimmer, a medal-winner, a public speaker, a TV presenter, a mum of two, and now an author. This book is a fun-filled guide to disabilities, and it's an invitation for you to ask questions, start conversations and learn about each other.

When I was at school, I remember learning the alphabet. I don't remember being taught about disability, diversity or the importance of real inclusion. These are lessons I've had to learn myself, and they're lessons I want to share with the world. One in five Australians lives with a disability, and the disability community is wide and varied, big and beautiful, bold and bright, and has a great sense of pride.

Sometimes you can see the disabilities people have – such as short stature (me!), cerebral palsy or paraplegia. Then there are the disabilities that can't be seen, such as low vision and chronic pain, and cognitive disabilities such as ADHD and autism.

Everyone's experience with disability is different, and the severity of a person's disability can change from day to day. Of course, these visible and invisible disabilities are just a few examples. You'll learn about other disabilities in the following pages, and there's also much more to learn outside of this book.

People have different preferences about what they're called, and what they call themselves – a "disabled person" or a "person with a disability". Most prefer for the word "person" to come before the word "disability". Some say they're "disabled" first because it's part of their identity. There's no shame in being disabled, after all. The thing to know is that one person's preference might not be another's. I always refer to a person by their name and not their disability.

It's natural to be curious, to want to ask questions and to learn about someone new. But always be respectful and remember: disability isn't a dirty word.

In this book you'll read about different disabilities, discover new words and hopefully learn a thing or two (or three or four). Words matter, and I believe the words in these pages are worth knowing, but there are so many other words to learn, too.

I hope this book is just the start of understanding the world of disabilities, but if you take one thing away after reading it, I would love it to be this: our differences are what make us special, they're a part of our individual uniqueness and they make the world a better, more interesting place.

Happy reading, you legends!

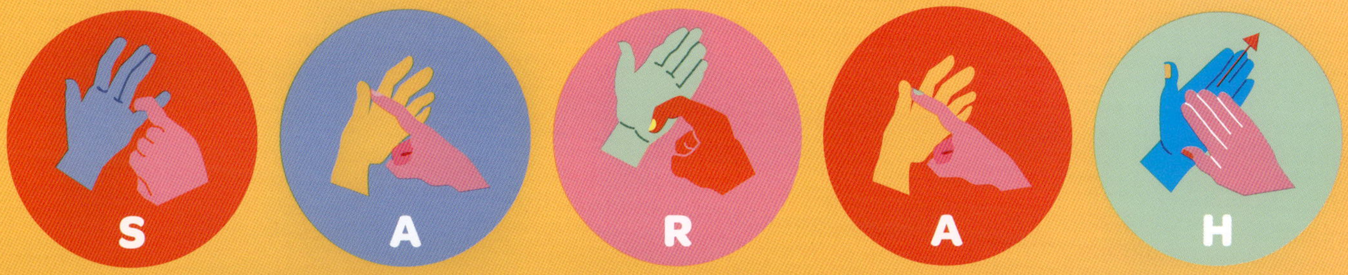

Follow along to learn the Auslan alphabet!

A is for **ability**

Can you touch your toes?
Can you strike a pose?
Can you tie your shoelaces in bows?

We all have different **abilities** that make us unique. It's nice to focus on the things we can do rather than the things we can't – but it's important to remember there's nothing wrong with having a disability. Being disabled doesn't make you less, it just makes you different. Disability doesn't mean inability. We're all different, and we're all a little bit magic!

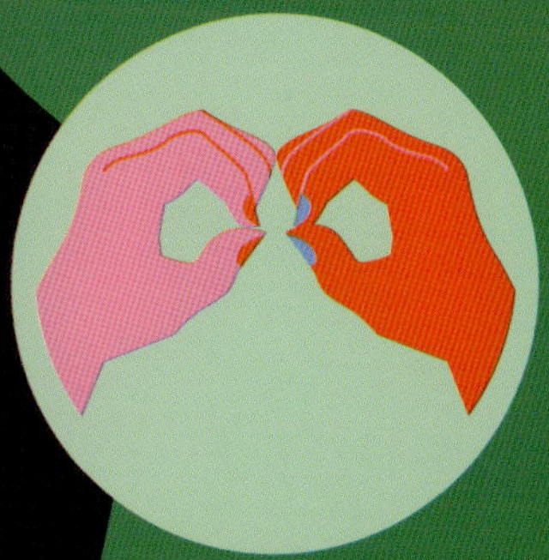

B is for brain injuries

How many stars are in the Milky Way galaxy? Oh, about the same number of neurons we have in our brains. That's around 100 billion!

Just like the stars in the sky, every brain is unique. Around 700,000 Australians have an acquired **brain injury** (ABI). A brain injury includes any damage to the brain that occurs after birth, such as accidents, falls, strokes, infections, or diseases like Parkinson's, and it can affect how we move, think and communicate.

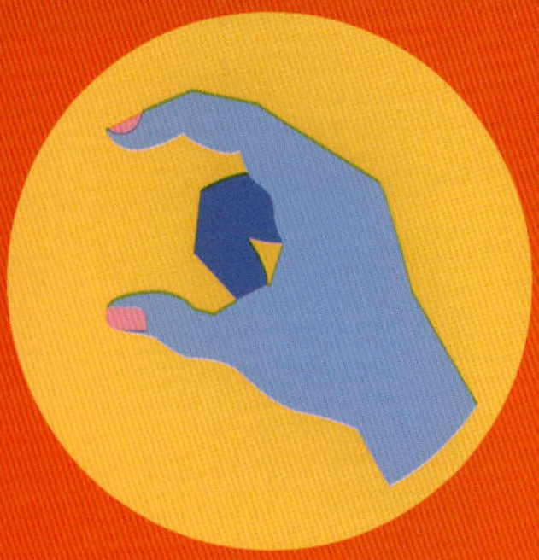

C is for cerebral palsy

Our brains control our muscles, how we move and how we groove.

Cerebral palsy is the most common motor disability in childhood and the condition can affect movement and muscle tone or posture. Even though people with cerebral palsy can have floppy or rigid limbs, that doesn't stop them from getting their groove on.

D is for dwarfism

They say good things come in small packages. I say good things come in short packages.

Dwarfism is a condition characterised by short stature and caused by a genetic or medical condition. I was born with dwarfism, and I'm proud to be a little person. It's okay to say "dwarf", "little person" and "person of short stature", but it is most respectful to use people's names. You can call me Sarah, Sar, or legend!

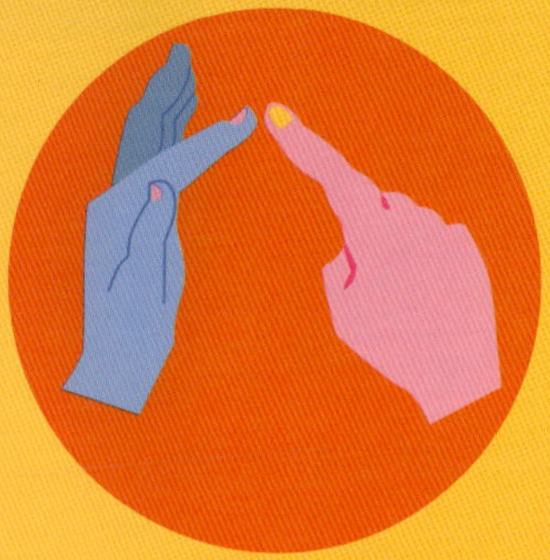

E is for **epilepsy**

Nerves can make our stomachs somersault, our knees knock and our tongues twist.

When the nerves in our brain are disrupted, it can cause seizures. **Epilepsy** is a brain disorder where a person experiences repeated seizures, which can cause jerking movements, shaking and confusion. When someone has a seizure it's important to stay calm, keep them safe, support their head and stay with them.

F is for **friendship**

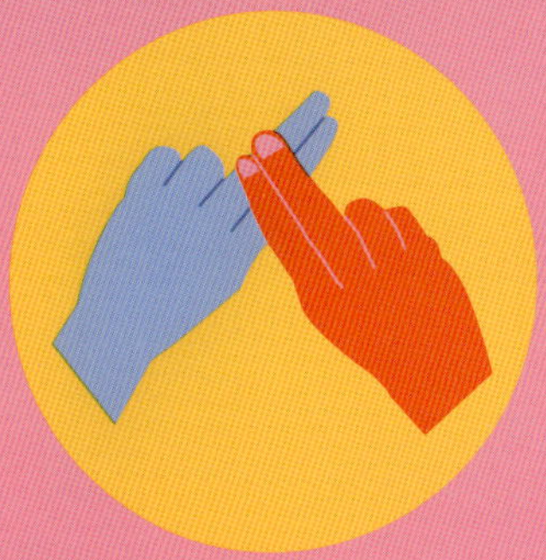

What's the strongest ship in the world? Friend-ship!

Real **friends** are there for us. They cheer us on when we're riding high and cheer us up when we're feeling down. Making friends isn't always easy, but being a friend is the greatest thing you can be. What makes you a good friend? Do you include others in games, do you high-five your friend for being brave, do you listen to them when they talk? That's what friends are for.

G is for **genetic disorders**

Jeans can be tight, and they can be bright. They can sit on your hips, and they can get rips.

We can change the style of jeans we wear, but we can't change the genes we are born with. **Genetic disorders** – such as cystic fibrosis, Huntington's disease and Down syndrome – are health conditions caused by a difference in someone's DNA. For example, Down syndrome happens when a person has an extra – bonus – chromosome. Children with Down syndrome can grow, develop and learn at a different pace, but all good things take time.

H is for **hard of hearing**

Ears are good for tucking hair behind, for holding sunglasses and for wearing sparkly earrings.

Deafness can be caused by genetics, and it can also develop in childhood and later life for many different medical reasons. Communicating with Australian Sign Language (Auslan), which uses hand gestures and body movements instead of sound, just like the illustrations on these pages, is used widely, and cochlear implants and lip reading can also be of great benefit. And for those of us who are **hard of hearing**, hearing aids really help!

I is for **invisible disability**

**We can't see the wind, but we can feel it.
We can't touch the air, but we can breathe it.**

We can't see all disabilities – some are invisible, such as autism and dyslexia. These are a couple of examples of the many invisible disabilities that exist. Even though **invisible disabilities** may not be immediately obvious to others, that doesn't make them any less real – just like the wind and the air.

J

is for **joints**

We can push, we can pull, and we can point – all thanks to our joints.

A **joint** is the part of the body where two or more bones meet to allow movement. Our joints can become inflamed, infected and injured. The most common cause of joint pain is arthritis, which is the inflammation, swelling and tenderness of one or more joints and can affect kids, teenagers and older people alike.

K is for **kindness**

If you're counting numbers at school, swimming in the pool or sitting on a stool, being kind is always cool.

Disabled people don't want special treatment. We don't want a gold trophy or a sparkly VIP badge. We just want to be treated with respect and **kindness** – like everyone does. In a world where you can be anything you want, be kind.

L is for (prosthetic) limbs

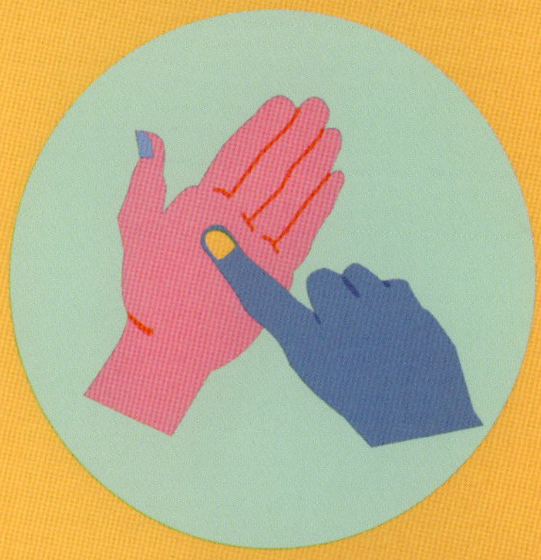

Legs can be long, they can be short, they can have freckles and they can even be made of metal.

Prosthetic limbs can be used to replace missing arms or legs. They can help people to walk, eat, get dressed and jump out of bed. Basic artificial limbs such as wooden legs and hooks for hands have been used since 600 BC. Today's versions are much lighter, more comfortable and functional.

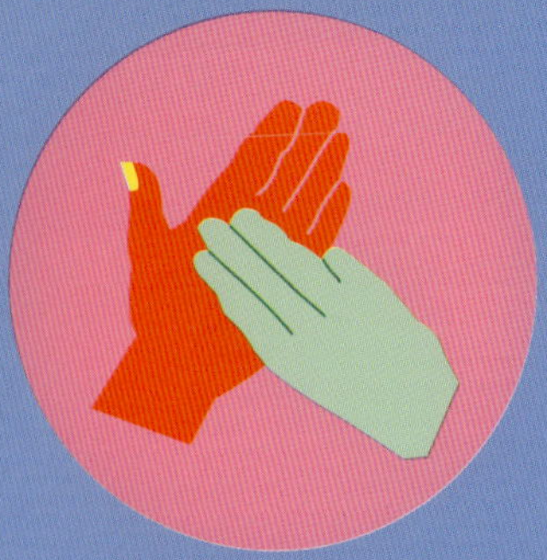

M is for **mental health**

Jogging and jumping, skipping and skating, dancing and diving can help us stay fit – in our bodies and our minds.

Just as important as our physical health is our **mental health**. Everyone can feel sad, stressed and upset sometimes. In these times, be kind to your mind. Take three deep breaths, feel your feet on the floor, talk to someone you trust and always remember you are not alone.

N is for neurodiverse

Did you know the human brain can generate enough power to run a lightbulb?

Our brains are amazing, and they're all different. **Neurodiversity** is an umbrella word used to explain the unique ways our brains work. Under this umbrella there is autism, attention-deficit/hyperactivity disorder (ADHD), dyslexia, Tourette syndrome and dyscalculia, which affect how we learn and process information. It's important to remember that there is no one, "right" way of thinking, learning or feeling.

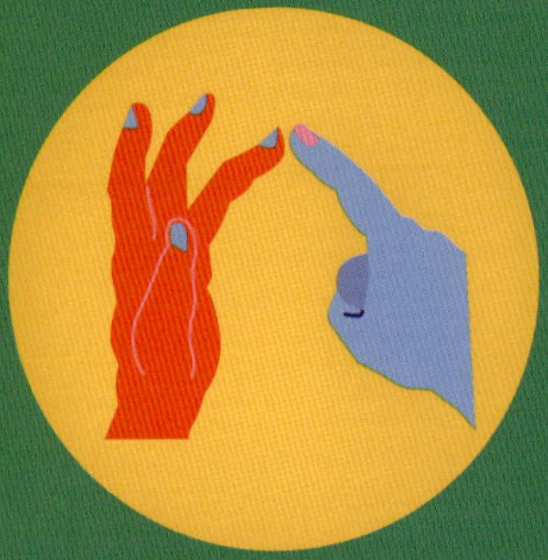

O is for **obstacles**

Obstacles can get in our way, they can cause a delay and they can make us go the long way, but they can't hold us down.

Obstacles are a part of life. We all face them, but for those of us with a disability, obstacles can be more challenging and more frequent, making them more exhausting! Obstacles can be physical, such as steep stairs, and social, such as discrimination. When obstacles are removed, disabled people can live a more fulfilled life. Let's clear the way for all of us for a brighter future.

P is for **Paralympians**

Be bold, break the mould and go for gold!

Just like the Olympics, the **Paralympics** are for athletes at the top of their game. Elite athletes with a disability from all around the world compete in sports including wheelchair basketball, badminton, table tennis, taekwondo, shot-put and swimming, to name a few. What's your favourite sport to play? What sport would you like to try?

Q is for **quadriplegic**

Quad means four. Quadruplets are four babies. A quad bike has four wheels...

And a **quadriplegic** person is someone affected by paralysis of all four of their limbs: their legs and arms. A paraplegic person is someone who has paralysis of the legs, but not the arms. Quadriplegics may require support with daily tasks such as eating, getting dressed, bathing and moving.

R

is for **respect**

There are so many ways to say g'day to your mates! You can wave, high-five or offer a hug hello.

Not everyone likes to be touched so it's important to **respect** each other's personal space. And not everyone likes loud noises so it's also important to be sensitive about sound. For those on the autism spectrum or who have ADHD or a sensory processing disorder, being touched or greeted loudly can be triggering. Being conscious around someone who is wearing noise-cancelling headphones or who stiffens when they're touched is respectful – and much appreciated.

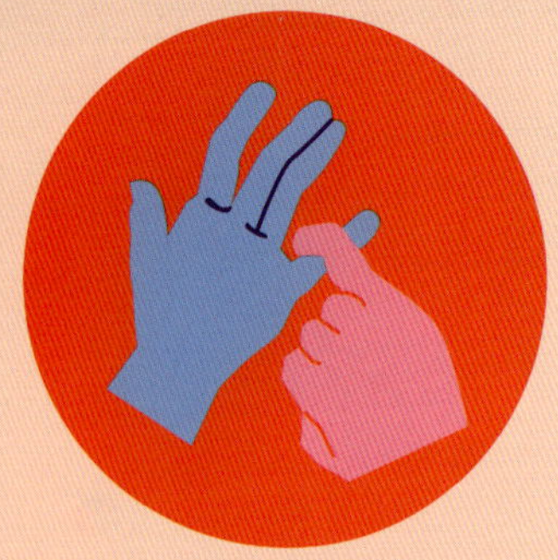

S is for **spina bifida**

Spines can come in all shapes and sizes: they can be straight or curved, long or short, stiff or stretchy.

Spina bifida is a disorder that occurs when a baby's backbone doesn't form properly before they are born. Treatment options can include having surgery, wearing a back brace and doing physical therapy. There is no cure for spina bifida, but there is support.

T is for **talk**

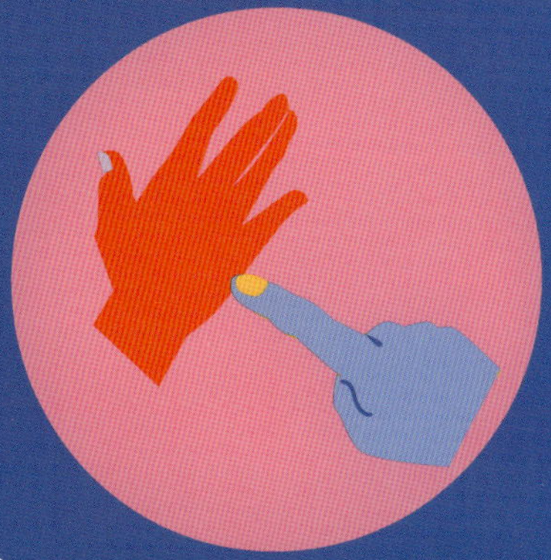

Have a chat, spin a yarn, jibber-jabber.

Someone with an acquired brain injury (ABI) may speak slowly or use a communication aid such as voice-to-text on their phone or computer. Someone with cluttering – a speech disorder – may talk fast, and someone with a stutter may pause, or repeat words and sounds. Some people communicate differently, but you can communicate with them in a way you can both share. When you **talk** to someone with a disability, be yourself, ask questions, listen to the answers and always be respectful.

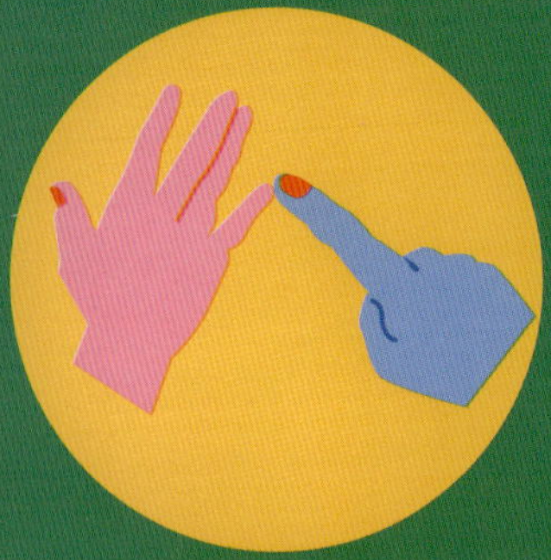

U is for **unique**

What's something every single person has in common? We're all unique, of course!

Even identical twins have different fingerprints. There's nothing wrong with being different, standing out or shining bright. Our **uniqueness** is something to be embraced and celebrated – not embarrassed by. Can you think of something that sets you apart and makes you special?

V is for (low) vision

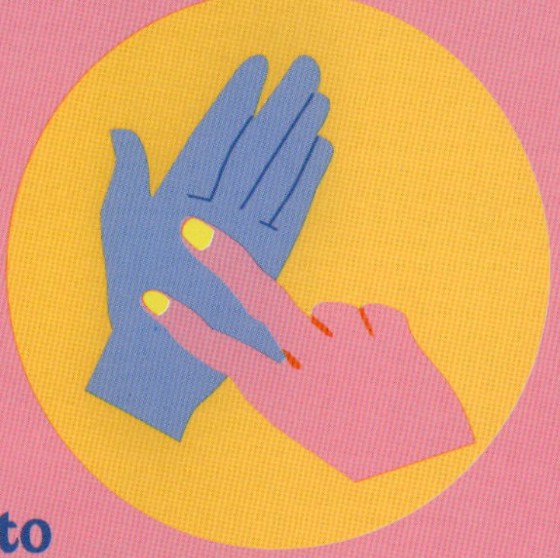

In the dark, outside in the park or trying to find a landmark, it helps to have some guidance.

For people with low vision, guidance can come in the form of magnifying glasses, white canes and service dogs. Guide dogs are working animals that are specially trained to help people who are blind or who have **low vision** to travel safely around their community. When service dogs are at work, we need to let them do their job, so it's good to remember not to pat or distract them (no matter how cute they might be!).

W is for **wheelchairs**

What goes around in circles but moves straight ahead? A wheel!

Wheelchairs (aka freedom machines!) help people with mobility issues to get around. When we talk about wheelchair users, we shouldn't say "wheelchair-bound" or "confined to a wheelchair", we should simply say "uses a wheelchair". Wheelchairs don't define people – and they don't confine people, either.

X is for **x-ray**

Say "cheeeeese!" With a camera, we can take photos of our faces, of our friends, and of our food. With an x-ray machine, we can take photos of our bones.

An **x-ray** takes pictures of bones and soft tissue to see what's happening inside. X-rays can detect broken bones, foreign objects and abnormal masses. Sometimes people might need to get an x-ray to check on their disability, or after an accident to determine the severity of their injury. X-rays can help us understand our insides if there's an issue that needs addressing.

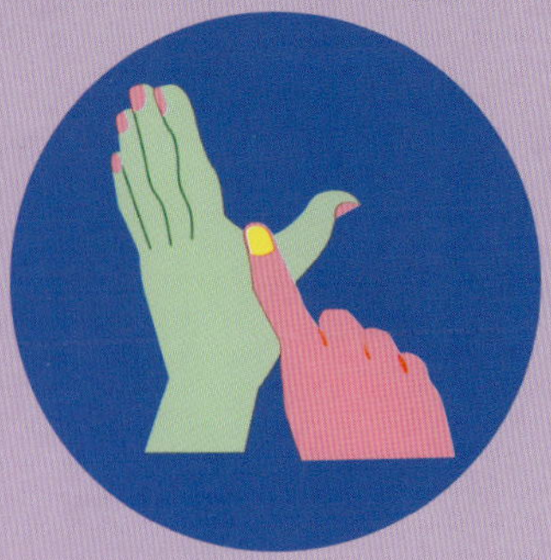

Y is for **yawning**

I yawn, you yawn, we all yawn together. Yawning can be contagious like smiling and giggling uncontrollably.

People with disabilities – and especially those with chronic fatigue syndrome – can get tired easily and need to rest. Sleep helps us all to heal, reduce stress and think more clearly. Does that make you want to crawl into bed? You're in luck, because ...

Z is for **zzz**

That's it! We've made it, we're at the very end.

Now we've learned the alphabet – and so many new words – it's time for us to rest. Sleep tight, sweet dreams, nighty night. Let's do this again. Until then, keep learning, stay politely curious, and remember to celebrate what makes you different.

A Lothian Children's Book
Published in Australia and New Zealand in 2024
by Hachette Australia
Gadigal Country, Level 17, 207 Kent Street, Sydney, NSW 2000
www.hachettechildrens.com.au

Hachette Australia acknowledges and pays our respects to the past, present and future Traditional Owners and Custodians of Country throughout Australia and recognises the continuation of cultural, spiritual and educational practices of Aboriginal and Torres Strait Islander peoples. Our head office is located on the lands of the Gadigal people of the Eora Nation.

NATIONAL LIBRARY OF AUSTRALIA
A catalogue record for this book is available from the National Library of Australia

ISBN: 978 0 7344 2302 3 (hardback)

Designed by Liz Seymour
Colour reproduction by Splitting Image
Printed in China by Toppan Leefung Printing Limited